BUNNY MONEY

BUNNY MONEY

ROSEMARY WELLS

PUFFIN BOOKS

For Ann Tobias

PUFFIN BOOKS
Published by the Penguin Group
Penguin Putnam Books for Young Readers, 345 Hudson Street, New York, New York 10014, U.S.A.
Penguin Books Ltd, 27 Wrights Lane, London W8 5TZ, England
Penguin Books Australia Ltd, Ringwood, Victoria, Australia
Penguin Books Canada Ltd, 10 Alcorn Avenue, Toronto, Ontario, Canada M4V 3B2
Penguin Books (N.Z.) Ltd, 182-190 Wairau Road, Auckland 10, New Zealand

Penguin Books Ltd, Registered Offices: Harmondsworth, Middlesex, England

First published in the United States of America by Dial Books for Young Readers,
a division of Penguin Books USA Inc., 1997
Published by Puffin Books, a division of Penguin Putnam Books for Young Readers, 2000

44

Copyright © Rosemary Wells, 1997
All rights reserved

THE LIBRARY OF CONGRESS HAS CATALOGED THE DIAL EDITION AS FOLLOWS:
Wells, Rosemary.
Bunny Money / by Rosemary Wells.—1st ed.
p. cm.
"A Max and Ruby picture book."
Summary: Max and Ruby spend so much on emergencies while shopping for
Grandma's birthday presents that they just barely have enough money left for gifts.
ISBN 0-8037-2146-3 (trade)—ISBN 0-8037-2147-1 (lib.)
(1. Shopping—Fiction. 2. Money—Fiction. 3. Brothers and sisters—Fiction.
4. Rabbits—Fiction 5. Grandmothers—Fiction.) I. Title.
PZ7.W46843Bv 1997b [E]—dc20 96-24570 CIP AC

Puffin Books ISBN 978-0-14-056750-2

Manufactured in China

The artwork for each picture is an ink drawing with watercolor painting.

Max's sister, Ruby, saved up a walletful of money for
Grandma's birthday present.

"We're going to buy Grandma a music box with skating ballerinas, Max," said Ruby. "Get your lucky quarter and let's go shopping!"

Ruby took one dollar

from her wallet to pay the bus fare.

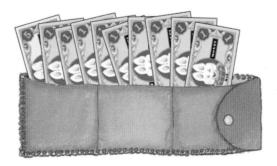

The bus stopped at Rosalinda's Gift Shop.

In the window was a music box with skating ballerinas.

"Isn't it beautiful, Max!" said Ruby.

"Thirsty," said Max.

"You may buy a very, very small lemonade, Max," said Ruby.

Next door in Candi's Corner window were hundreds of vampire teeth.

Max knew Grandma would love a set of teeth with oozing cherry syrup inside for her birthday.

He bought them instead of the lemonade.

"Two dollars, please," said Candi.

Max wanted to make sure the teeth worked.

He put them in.

The teeth worked perfectly.

Ruby had to take Max to the Laundromat.

 Soap cost a dollar.

 The washer cost a dollar.

 And the dryer cost another dollar.

"Money down the drain, Max," said Ruby.

"Hungry!" said Max.

It was lunchtime.

Max finished off a peanut butter and jelly sandwich,

two coconut cupcakes,   and a banana shake.

Lunch cost four dollars.

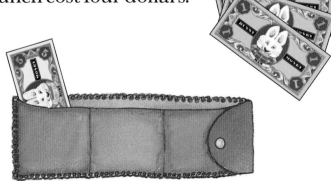

"Money is running through our fingers, Max," said Ruby.

They walked all the way back to Rosalinda's Gift Shop without spending another penny.

"I'd like to buy the music box with skating ballerinas for Grandma's birthday," Ruby said to Rosalinda.

"It's a hundred dollars," said Rosalinda.

"A hundred dollars!" said Ruby.

"The ice skates are made of real gold," Rosalinda explained.

Ruby looked in her wallet. The only thing left was a five-dollar bill.

"Here's an idea!" said Rosalinda. "Bluebird earrings that play

'Oh, What a Beautiful Morning!' are on sale for four dollars. Gift

wrap is free."

"We'll take them," said Ruby.

Ruby gave Rosalinda the five-dollar bill

for the bluebird earrings

and went to pick out wrapping paper.

"Four dollars for the earrings . . . one dollar change!" said

Rosalinda. "You take care of this dollar, young man!"

Max went back to Candi's Corner. Glow-in-the-dark vampire teeth were half price.

"Most people like Glow-in-the-dark vampire teeth much better than the oozing cherry kind," said Candi.

Max bought a set

for one dollar.

"Oh, no, Max," said Ruby. "You've spent our last dollar.

How are we going to pay for the bus home?"

Max reached into his pocket. Out came his lucky quarter.
Ruby used it for the telephone.
"Grandma will have to pick us up," said Ruby. "I hope she
won't be angry."

Grandma was not angry at all.

She was so thrilled, she played the musical bluebird earrings

and wore the vampire teeth all the way home.

Making Money!

If you want to go shopping with Max and Ruby,

you will need plenty of Bunny Money.

Ask a grown-up to help you photocopy the money

that is inside the front and back covers of this book.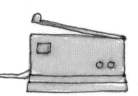

 Then, with a grown-up's help, cut out

the money you have photocopied and

paste the fronts to the backs

(plain sides together).

You can color your money

if you like.

Happy shopping!

JONAS SALK

MOTHER HALE

MAHATMA GANDHI

YO-YO MA

JESSYE NORMAN

MARIE CURIE

MARTINA NAVRATILOVA

JULIA CHILD

ELEANOR ROOSEVELT

FRIDA KAHLO

DESMOND TUTU

JANE AUSTEN

CHIEF SEATTLE

RACHEL CARSON

FRED ASTAIRE

JESSE OWENS